FOR DAWS TO PECK AT

AMONG THE MYTHOS BOOK 4

RUTHANNE REID

CONTENTS

Copyright

Copyright © 2019 by **Ruthanne Reid**

All rights reserved. No part of this publication may be reproduced, distributed or transmitted in any form or by any means, without prior written permission.

NO AI TRAINING: Without in any way limiting the author's exclusive rights under copyright, any use of this publication to "train" generative artificial intelligence (AI) technologies to generate text is expressly prohibited. The author reserves all rights to license uses of this work for generative AI training and development of machine learning language models.

www.ruthannereid.com

Publisher's Note: This is a work of fiction. Names, characters, places, and incidents are a product of the author's imagination. Locales and public names are sometimes used for atmospheric purposes. Any resemblance to actual people, living or dead, or to businesses, companies, events, institutions, or locales is completely coincidental.

For Daws to Peck At/ Ruthanne Reid. – 1st ed.

✝ HUMAN AUTHORED

Reg #: 9052032, https://authorsguild.org/human

Formatted using Lacuna

For Bennett, who reminded me gazpacho is best served cold.

"Natural selection, as it has operated in human history, favors not only the clever but the murderous."

——Barbara Ehrenreich

CHAPTER 1

CHILDREN OF THE NIGHT

Vampires do not grow old, nor do they sicken. They heal from injuries quickly—at least, when they have something good and red to drink—and never do they simply languish.

This was just one reason why Jonathan was strange.

In no one's memory had he been *well*. They'd tried everything to help him—favors called in, deductive spellwork used, and dietary changes enacted—but nothing helped. It was as though Father's blood fought something inside him, something that didn't quite manage the transformation to Night-Child the way things were supposed to go, and the resulting carnage left Jonathan's body frail. He was practically the traditional cursed prince, ailing until someone, somewhere, could provide him with a curing kiss.

At least there was nothing wrong with his mind. Whoever educated him had been thorough, and he spoke a dozen languages, and he played a dozen instruments, and he wielded a paintbrush with skill that echoed Bosch or Dong Yuan. He was nice; he was thoughtful; he was also clearly dying, albeit agonizingly slowly, and his adopted family of the Blood didn't know what to do.

"All I'm saying is, has anybody taken him to a regular doctor, like?" said Liza distractedly, and tossed the black-handled dirk into the air.

"Sure," said Terrance, sprawled on the sofa like a melting teenager and staring grimly at the ceiling. "Did nothing. They couldn't tell nobody nothing about us, anyway."

Liza tossed the dirk again, fascinated by its shine, more fascinated by the way her new sight could follow it and her new hands could catch it every time, every time.

Terrance sighed. "Sorry, love. Didn't mean to drop this on your head, you being young, and all."

Liza laughed. "We're family, right? It's good to not hide things from me because I'm young, or so said Arabelle."

Terrance shrugged slightly, his leather jacket creaking with the movement. "You didn't see Da' leave Jonathan's room this morning. I know him, Da'. He was concerned. Real concerned. And now he's off, and Roderick's in charge, but he's not paying attention to the details like a brother who's always sick and might be getting sicker."

Liza stopped tossing and stared at him. "Sounds to me like you think Roderick's botching it."

"Well, it won't be the first time I've thought that," said Terrance, his Irish lilt abruptly stronger. Rogue-like, he peeked at her sidelong and winked, green eyes dangerous, thin lips sensual and somehow far from safe. But then his gaze turned inward again, and he looked away.

How bizarre.

Liza knew who Terrance was, of course; Father's *knife*, the assassin, the hard hand beneath the silk glove, the only member of Notte's family to actually kill people on the regular.

Well, tonight, he was apparently killing time, and he'd slunk in here, plopped on the sofa, and started talking.

She didn't have a role like *knife* yet. Her Beast was just under control, enough that she was permitted to roam the halls instead of staying safely tucked in the Newbie Night-Child rooms. All things being logical, she wasn't sure why Terrance was telling her this.

Maybe because she brought with her a talent these older magical beings often forgot: pragmatism. "So what do you want to do about him, then? Jonathan, I mean," she said.

Terrance sighed. "There's nothing."

"No," said Liza patiently, and handed him back his dirk. She sat next to him, not bothering to adjust skirt or halter top because intimacy meant new things these days and nip-slips no longer mattered. "You've come in here, presented a problem, and now you're frozen. No good, mate. We have the issue. What are we going to do about it?"

"It's 'we' now, is it?" said Terrance, the rogue's grin making a return.

"I'm family now, right? Blood," she said. "It's already *we*. And you didn't answer my question."

They didn't look like blood. Terrance was all pale and scattered freckles, lanky and sharp and orange. She was dark and shapely (a word Arabelle had used and she liked very much), her kinky afro bigger than Terrance's whole body, and there wasn't a sharp place on her body except for very particular teeth.

But they were blood. It was found family and *made* family, a strange and glorious weaving, and nothing would change that now.

"Well, I guess we could run him through all the tests again, or drag some member of the Sun in here to see if they could heal him, but that's been done," said Terrance. "Nobody even knows what's wrong. He's a medical mystery, he is."

Liza sat back, studying the ceiling beside him. All problems presented a solution eventually when looked at the right way. She held her hands up as though miming some sort of cube, turning it to see different sides.

Eyes lidded, Terrance watched her.

"Well," said Liza after a moment. "Anybody asked him?"

"Asked who?" said a voice from the doorway, and in came Salome, literally butting her way inside as her hands were occupied with a large tray.

"Jonathan," said Liza promptly, because she liked Salome, respected Salome, maybe a little bit wanted Salome, which was only to be expected.

"Oh, he's a mess," said Salome, and didn't smile because she never did. If Terrance was aping a 1950s look and Liza liked playing in the 1970s, Salome chose to stay where she'd been *made*, back in the roaring 20s, and her drop-waist dress and pageboy haircut might as well have been created for her waifish self.

"Said as much," said Terrance.

"I need you to sniff this," said Salome, holding up the tray on which she'd balanced a dozen little ramekins with clear liquid. "New scents I'm testing."

Leaving Terrance spread like miserable peanut butter on the sofa, Liza got up to sample, sniffing delicately over the tray. "This one. I really like this one."

"Bergamot and wild orange as a base. Never fails," said Salome. "So you want to ask Jonathan what's wrong?"

"Well, yeah," said Liza, leaning on her east London accent. "Has anybody actually tried that yet?"

"Sure," said Terrance, then frowned. "Probably."

"*You* didn't," said Liza. "I know I didn't—I barely met him beyond the welcoming ceremony."

Salome shrugged. "I didn't, either."

"Well, that cinches it," said Liza. "I say we go. I say we go right now and ask the bloke if he has any inkling what's wrong."

There was a moment of silence, and then Terrance moved.

He didn't stand like an ordinary person. He slid like a blade from a sheath, rose like blood in a wound, and his playful tone didn't fit. "Field trip it is, then."

"Eh, might as well." Salome put her tray on the coffee table. "Father's gone, anyway, so it's boring. Roderick is boring."

Terrance smirked, suddenly intense and dangerous as a hunting dog. "That's why Roddy's in charge. Boring people don't rock the boat."

And then they were going, walking with purpose through the manor as if on mission. Well, that was easy, Liza thought with some surprise. Who knew? Maybe they could actually do some good.

CHAPTER 2

JONATHAN

Night-Children were all connected.

Father called it the *skein*: one thread tying them all together, linked unbroken through the thick wool of their family to its core. The older ones could feel one another if they tried, find one another across vast distances, for all that it was a vague and watery connection.

Apparently, Father's connection was not watery, and he felt every single Night-Child intensely, all the time.

It sounded like a nightmare to Liza. Her maker had told her that making a Night-Child was like sacrificing part of your brain, and that part experienced your new child's joy and your new child's pain forever. It could not be switched off.

That was quite a commitment, and it could grow. If Liza ever chose to make a Night-Child, Arabelle would be aware of that person in the same way.

Liza had no desire to make a Night-Child.

Still, the whole thing had its uses. Right now, for example, Terrance knew exactly where Jonathan was.

She followed her two older siblings deep into Notte's magically expanded manor, past the largely empty rooms for newbie vamps, past the weird spaces populated by misty, bow-tied ghosts dusting artworks, past the vaults of vast uncounted treasure, and into Notte's personal halls.

Up here, only the first-born slept. These were rooms for Night-Children Notte had made himself, which at present numbered eight.

Or maybe nine. Jonathan must have been first-born because he was here, leaning in his doorway, waiting for them.

There he stood, ethnicity undetermined, green eyes slanted, his lips too full to swing him into handsome. He looked like a stiff breeze could destroy him, his olive skin made pale by his silk and mahogany surroundings. The simple Mandarin-collared suit he wore failed to hide how thin he'd become.

In spite of that, he was so pretty that Liza felt the puerile urge to touch him.

Terrance slowed. "Didn't expect to see you up," he said carefully. "You waiting for something?"

"Thank you for coming," Jonathan replied as though he'd requested their presence. He glanced up at Liza, straight black hair hanging into his eyes, and she suddenly knew he'd expected her, expected all of them.

A strange dizziness came with this, light, barely there, as if the train she rode had tilted on its track.

He looked at her, his long fingers clutching at one another restlessly, his gaze steady. He was waiting for her to respond. *Her.*

Why?

Liza clenched her jaw. Her grandmother had not raised her to spook this easily, damn it. "I'm here," she said.

"Thank you." Relief slumped Jonathan's shoulders, and when he looked down, his long lashes lay like full black brush strokes against his cheeks. "Please come in."

"Lay it on thick, why don'tcha," Terrance muttered, but accepted Jonathan's waved invitation to his room.

It was large and lavish, as was much of Notte's home—romanticized by default, tapestries competing with a canopy bed for revisited Gothic glory. The only part Jonathan had personalized was the space he used for painting.

Easels and canvases filled that corner of the wood-paneled room, stacked and wrapped in oil cloth, surrounded by paints and palettes like foothills. One easel stood under a recessed spotlight, dust-motes floating around it as though it had been recently moved.

The dizzy feeling increased, a sense of tilting, and Liza didn't want him to remove that oil cloth. Whatever was under it would change things, important and crucial things, but she couldn't speak or stop the weird inertia of these moments.

Salome pressed past Liza, looking around, and sniffed twice. "You haven't had a human in here in weeks," she accused.

Jonathan looked down again, reddened. "I haven't. I'm sorry."

"What, you're not eating?" blurted Liza, saying anything to avoid the removal of drop cloths and presuppositions. "Is that what's wrong? That's all that's wrong with you, that you can't or won't drink blood?" But she knew it wasn't that simple, and her words were blades of grass on the train-tracks, mowed down.

Jonathan glanced at her. "I'm sorry."

"You keep saying that. Sorry for what?" said Terrance carefully, no longer smiling.

Jonathan took a deep breath and pulled the drop cloth off the spot-lit easel.

Liza's face, Terrance's, and Salome's featured on three cubist bodies, clearly running or fighting or in some mad action. Distress stretched their eyes and mouths like caverns, and behind them loomed a huge structure in angry black and gray. Blood shocked everywhere in spills and splashes, but the worst thing was the man in the forefront of the painting, the man stretched out like a Medieval rack victim, the man flayed, torn, savaged open like a mad bear's prey.

Pieces of him peppered the canvas, leaving trails and stains and droplets, and Liza suddenly realized her painted self was trodding over severed fingers, and painted Terrance clutched a ruined heart in his hand, and painted

Salome danced in horror, arching in some terrible tripping ecstasy even as she tried to run away.

If Liza moved at all, if she even shifted from foot to foot, the shading on the painted heart made it twitch in Terrance's hand like a crushed kitten.

All of this hit her in less than a second, like a slap, like a hammer, and she suddenly had to vomit.

Jonathan's bathroom was pristine. She tried not to make a mess.

They'd waited for her before continuing. "All right," said Terrance after the rinsing and spitting was done. "I think maybe you want to explain this."

Jonathan sat heavily on a plush armchair. "I'm sorry. I would have asked you earlier, but it wasn't *time* yet, and he's suffered so much." His voice broke.

Me, Liza thought because she couldn't avoid it. *He was waiting for me to be ready,* and the train tilted its way off the tracks and began rumbling like catastrophe through the countryside.

Salome leaned in. "This canvas smells like blood."

"It's mine," said Jonathan softly. "I mix it in. It helps, sometimes."

"You're bleeding *and* not drinking? So nasty," said Salome with appreciation, studying the canvas.

"He sees the future when he paints," said Terrance too calmly to be teasing, too casually to be making a joke.

Liza looked at him. "The future."

"Yep."

"Wouldn't that be magic?" she said.

"Yep."

This felt like some weird test. "Magic-users can't become Night-Children. This is basic," she said.

"Yep," agreed Terrance, adding a shrug as if to say, *What's a guy to do?*

"I'm sorry," Jonathan said again. "I know this is a lot."

"It isn't yet," said Terrance. "But we're getting there, aren't we?"

"I don't know why it worked for me." Jonathan looked down again, folding his hands. "Nobody does."

Liza straightened her spine. "Do I have this right? You want me to believe this . . . painting is our future?"

"You all make it out safely," said Jonathan, looking up at her suddenly and pleadingly. "None of that blood is yours. It's *his* blood, all of it is *his*, and he doesn't have much time left."

"His?" said Salome.

"His name—" began Jonathan, but got no further because Terrance began to swear.

It wasn't a language Liza knew, but some words are unmistakable regardless of etymology.

"All right, there?" drawled Salome after some time had passed.

"That's *her sword!*" Terrance said, pointing at the canvas. "That's who's laid out like a run-over rabbit, isn't it? *Isn't it?*"

"Yes," said Jonathan.

Terrance began swearing again, accompanied with pacing.

"I don't understand," Liza said, a careful understatement.

"He's a murderer. A thug. A bully."

"Fine words from Father's *knife,*" said Salome, giving him a hard look. "We all got blood on our hands, you old hypocrite." She knelt in front of Jonathan. "Why are you showing us this? Do you want us to do something?"

"Yes. You're the three who save him," he said simply.

"Why and how?"

"*Wait,*" interrupted Liza, speaking louder, trying to drown out the rumble of runaway train. "Nobody can see the future. It's statistically impossible. There are too many variables!"

"You're missing the point, love," said Terrance.

Liza spun on him. "So instruct me, *brother.*"

"Then let's lay it out!" Warning suddenly darkened Terrance's tone, made his eyes flash, and he raised his arms in expressive rage. "Here's how it works. We *eat* humans and *come from* humans. We don't matter to the rest of the magic-using Mythos because *this doesn't apply to them*—and yet here we are, facing someone human enough to be *made*, but still magic enough to tell the future." He looked at her. "Might be something nobody else needs to know, yeah? It'd be real bad if they found out. The Mythos might find reason to be scared, and scared people do dangerous things."

Liza stared at him.

"I'm sorry," Jonathan said so gently. "I don't control the future. I just see where the threads go. If I'd said nothing, you'd still end up over there *because she'd ask for you*, but it would be worse, and harder, because you wouldn't know you'll be all right. I just . . . I wanted to make it easier for you. You're the three who save him, and I wanted to help how I could."

Liza made a sound of helpless disbelief, of balance dangerously threatened.

Jonathan met her gaze and held it, and she *saw*—saw weariness, sorrow, weight of years dragging through his soul like chains through wounded flesh, and she couldn't dismiss him, she couldn't just call him crazy or lying or proud. He was none of those things. He was sad, and tired, and she suddenly knew that if this were true, she wouldn't trade places with him for anything in the world.

"I'll repay you," Jonathan said slowly. "I'll repay all three of you. Here will be my gift: I'm going to paint you a scene from *your* future. I can't choose which one, or when. I can't control it. But it will be true, and it may help you someday."

"Wouldn't that change what I choose to do?" Liza managed, just as slowly. "Sort of invalidate itself?"

"It's more complicated than that," he said, and it was an apology, and it was a warning, and she was unsure if she wanted this gift or not.

"Shit," said Terrance in a cold and terrible voice. "Your maker is *her*, isn't it?"

Jonathan turned his face up, and the light swept his face like marble, arrested the room as if filled with a vision. "I saw you in a dream. I saw in the home of she who made me, and your arrival was so strange and so unexpected that when you asked for a favor, she gave it."

"*Her*." Terrance said the word again, turned as if he wanted to spit, then didn't because there was carpet.

"If you ask her to let you have him, she will do it," said Jonathan. "Please."

The future.

An accurate glimpse of the future, however brief.

It made no sense, but now Liza wanted it so badly she could taste it, feel it, as if her runaway train plummeted down a cliff.

"What's going to be asked of us?" said Salome.

"Things in line with who you are," said Jonathan. "Nothing you can't do easily. I promise."

"You could tell us. Warn us," said Terrance.

He shook his head. "It's kinder if I don't."

That sounded bad.

"Tell me you didn't set this up, lad," said Terrance. "Tell me you didn't scare Father and worry everybody to set this up."

Jonathan's eyes went wide. "No, I swear. I *can't* drink right now. I won't be able to until Seishirou comes to me. I promise I waited as long as I could." And here he looked at Liza again, as though her acceptance were the key.

She leaned against the wall, clinging to equilibrium, trying to wrest control of her life back from whatever this was.

Still looking at her, Jonathan touched the side of the canvas as tenderly as though the splatter of organs and blood were a person. "Please," he whispered.

Liza exhaled slowly. "How could anybody say no to that?" she said. "Course I'm in."

"All right," said Salome. "Wednesday's boring, anyway."

"Yeah," said Terrance, teeth bared. "Let's go to the dragon's den. Poke the devil and see if she eats us."

And internally, emotionally, Liza felt the train lurch onto another track, a new and solidly fastened way of spikes and ties, and barrel on toward an unexpected future as though that had always been the plan.

CHAPTER 3

RAVENA

Travel for the Night-Child involved unexplained quantum phenomena Father simply called *going to dust*.

At will, a Night-Child could disintegrate, become motes with awareness, and in that discorporated state, travel over land or sea or air.

It wasn't instantaneous, but it was fast. Dust was also what their bodies turned to the moment they died, but that was another subject.

Italy to England was an easy trip, and of course, Terrance knew exactly where they were going.

They reformed on a bare and rocky path, uneven granite slick with seaspray and draped in seaweed left over from high tide. At the end of the path, at the top of a hill, stood the estate from Jonathan's painting.

It was a dim blue distortion of Father's own. Notte had built a home of warm colors on the edge of the Mediterranean Sea, a repose of tawny limestone and deep red tiles. *She,* on the other hand, had gone for an unoccupied jut over the North Sea, for stone blues and grays, for asymmetrical arches and horror-movie alcoves just waiting to be filled with bats.

Liza slipped on some algae. "There a reason we didn't land closer?"

"It'd be saying we came to fight, not talk," said Terrance, who never slipped on anything. Hands in his pockets, he looked utterly relaxed, out for a lovely jaunt on slimy rocks above icy sea. "This way, walking up, where they could shoot at us if they wanted to, we're saying we aren't here as enemies."

"I . . . I thought we had a truce with her," said Liza quietly.

Terrance sighed, puffing out his cheeks.

"Truces can be complicated, little bat," said Salome behind her. "Just let us do the talking. We'll keep you safe."

"Don't promise what we can't guarantee. Nobody could protect us from Ravena of Monmouth except for Father, and *he's not here*," said Terrance.

They said nothing else until they reached the front door. Wind whistled over the gray heath, stealing heat and color.

The door was, of course, painted black.

"Should we get Father?" whispered Liza.

"If he were here, Ravena wouldn't cooperate at all," said Terrance, and knocked.

The door opened and light blazed.

Liza took a moment to translate what she saw: inside this gray, dismal place was a hive of blinding bright activity, white walls and floors and ceilings *objets d'art* to break it up.

Men and women—none of them human—walked briskly by, suits and skirts and heels a-clicking, but the one who held open the door was Liza's second impossibility of the day.

That was a kid.

A rude kid, judging by the disgusted look he gave them. A boy barely into puberty, and already *made*.

Liza stared. One didn't *make* children into Children. This was inviolable. This was not allowed.

The child, his existence a contradiction, didn't seem to think highly of his visitors. "What the hell are you lot doing here?"

"Lady in?" said Terrance as if they'd come to borrow sugar.

"Even if she was, why would she dick around with the likes of you?" said the boy who wasn't a boy, and then exaggeratedly looked Salome up and down like a popsicle on a hot day. "Now *you*, on the other hand, I can make time for."

"Sure. I've been looking for some good rat bait," said Salome, and smiled a warning.

The kid rolled his eyes.

Terrance leaned in. "Listen, roach, we got it on good authority that your lady needs some favors." He spread his arms, expansive and amicable except for his knife-sharp eyes. "We're here to help. Family, and all. Tell her what I said. She'll take it from there."

The boy rolled his eyes and slammed the door in their faces.

Liza rubbed her eyes. "That went well."

"Sure, it did. Nobody's shooting," said Terrance.

The wind moaned, sent debris chattering over the stairs, and slid up Liza's skirt like icy fingers. "So what now?"

"We wait until she shows herself," said Terrance grimly.

"You sure she's not just going to leave us out here like salesmen?"

"Oh, sure," said Salome. "She's probably watching us now. Ooh." She made a show of looking up and around and under each t-strap shoe.

This was going to take forever.

Liza wanted it over with, and it couldn't even get underway until *she* showed up. Sea-spray was making her hair stiff and her skin itch. This was not on. "So let's speed it up."

"I don't think we got a button to speed her up, love," said Terrance.

Liza raised her voice. "Come out, come out, wherever you are!"

Terrance gave her a slow *What the hell are you doing?* look.

"Well, she's Notte's oldest child, right? You'd think someone *that old* would mind other people's time a little better," said Liza, who knew this was teasing a tiger, who knew this was dangerous, and couldn't resist.

Salome looked fascinated.

"She'll have to make a show of us now, you know," said Terrance quietly.

"She was going to anyway, right? Or she wouldn't be making us stand out here in this fish-shit weather!" said Liza, louder still. "She's watching, other people are watching, so let's get this over with. Oy! Stop wasting our ti—"

Her last word died on her lips.

Power crashed into them like a wave.

It was a tsunami, drowning and crushing and controlling them completely, and all three sank to their knees without meaning to do it.

"Congratulations, you found her," Terrance managed, and clutched the front step as if to keep from being swept away.

Liza had, of course, met Notte. Everyone in line to be *made* had to meet Notte. If he didn't think you could cut it as a Night-Child, you didn't get made, and that's the way it was.

She'd thought it draconian at first, but that thought didn't last long.

Liza had never been sure if she found Notte wonderful or intimidating, sensual or crap-her-pants scary. He was so gentle-looking with his big curls and enviable lashes, with a face impossible to imagine ripping and tearing and taking blood and belonging to a monster.

But it did. And he was.

Choosing the life Arabelle offered seemed so simple until she met him—so Hollywood, so every-book-she-read when she was fifteen—and after that, seemed more like a terrifying life-choice that would infect her to her core, place her in a position and relationship she could never leave, and implant a ravening beast inside her, making her into a predator of the species she once was. There was no going back from this, and hungry immortality lasted an awful long time.

Notte's power was like that. It made her feel mortal, mouse-small, vulnerable. It was delicious and damning, pleasuring and petrifying, all at once.

Ravena's power was the same way, with one major difference: in her presence, Liza realized just how much Notte had been holding back in order to be kind.

Liza couldn't move. She'd sunk to her knees along with Salome and Terrance, and now she couldn't move.

No, she didn't *want* to move. That was the difference. All desire to resist this had shattered.

"Well, this is exciting," purred a voice, sliding over her like silk over naked breasts, and Liza shivered.

"Good to see you, Lady," said Terrance, sounding impossibly and impertinently normal in spite of clenched teeth and pale strain, and Liza managed to look up and see whom he was addressing.

"Oh," she said softly.

Ravena was beautiful. Stunning, actually, and she stunned even though she'd done nothing to make her presence pop. Subtle makeup blended her cheeks and lips, softening her darkly golden skin and the size of her green eyes. Her black hair was tied back in a tight bun, but the patterns against her skull showed it wildly curly. She'd dressed simply in a navy skirt and jacket, her shell-shirt a boring cream, and hadn't bothered with jewelry at all.

And Liza couldn't look away. The desire to lick this woman then lie at her feet drowned out rational thought.

"It's good to see you as well, knife," said Ravena, reminding Liza that an actual conversation was happening here. "And Salome, and . . . who is this?"

"Liza. She's new."

I am? thought Liza, growing aware of her own self once again.

She was stronger than this, damn it. She'd conquered her Beast, and she could conquer this. "Yeah," she said, her voice cracking. "I'm Liza. Made a couple years ago."

"And already walking around, in your own mind?" said Ravena so sweetly it couldn't possibly be sarcasm, her eyes wide, the unnatural green of her irises so dangerous.

Liza couldn't think of a way to respond.

"She's cool," said Salome. "We're all cool here. It's not an invasion, or anything."

"I assumed as much, or you'd be dead," said Ravena with honey and strychnine.

"We heard you needed some favors done," Terran pressed once more.

"What a funny thing to say! Who could have told you, in your family, that I needed some favors in mine?"

Liza couldn't take it. "Hey, I know crushing the newbie seems like fun and all, but could you maybe dial it back a bit? I can't think. You've got glue between my ears, and I hate it."

Ravena laughed.

A terrible moment teetered, doom on one side and relief on the other, and finally tipped to the favorable. "Adorable," Ravena said. "You may rise."

There was no *may* about it. Ravena meant *get up*, even as that molasses power pulled back from Liza's mind, freeing up the gears, bringing the revs down. Liza got up.

"Won't you please come in?" Ravena added.

Terrance grunted. "Let's get this over with," he said, and stalked inside, shoulders hunched toward his ears.

So this was the power of a fifteen-thousand-year-old vampire. Liza couldn't help wondering if she'd live long enough to exert power like that—and if she *could*, whether or not she'd behave the same way.

Was it, Liza wondered, possible to go crazy with so much sterile damn *white*?

It was eye-wateringly bright in here, like some old sci-fi idea of the future. The few post-modern concessions to creativity stopped twenty feet past the door, so they were apparently just to tell visitors that the inhabitants weren't crazy.

The inhabitants *were* crazy, though. Liza was certain.

They all wore outfits similar to Ravena's—super dull and professional, sleek and likely expensive, nary a shiny button or interesting tie to be found.

She and her siblings couldn't have looked more like aliens if they tried. Terrance slunk along in black leather and sulking, and Salome swayed like an escapee from a silent movie while the tiny beads on her dress sparkled like broken glass.

Liza felt like the intentional dash of color in some weird art film. There probably wasn't even a power cord here the orange of her halter top. What was wrong with these people? Couldn't they have fun? What was the point of living forever if you couldn't *play*?

"Join me," said Ravena in what was definitely not a request, and placed her hand on the wall.

An invisible door slid open.

"I don't usually entertain visitors," she added, crossing the (of course) white room to a wide desk—also white—set up near the far wall.

The far wall was entirely made of glass.

Beyond it stretched an enormous space of tine-swirled sand and baked-brown rocks, a Zen garden that filled the field of vision.

If that window looked out on the human world, Liza would eat her go-go boots.

Ravena sat down behind her desk and touched its surface. Immediately three squares slid open in the floor, and three chairs rose, all movements silent.

"Nice," said Terrance. "Soulless, but nice."

"I try," said Ravena. "We're all friends here. *Sit.*"

They sat. Or at least, Liza found herself in the left-most seat with no recollection of how she got there.

This junk was beginning to make her angry. The slight dizziness returned, train tilting again, threatening to turn wild and jump the tracks and maybe blow up on impact.

"So," said Ravena, lacing her fingers. "Why have you come?"

"Just what we said," drawled Salome, crossing her leg in a bizarrely insolent fashion. "We're here to do *you* three favors, and in return, we just want one. Pretty good deal."

Ravena smiled widely, her lips tightly closed. "That all depends on what's being asked, doesn't it?"

Salome started to answer, but Terrance held up his hand.

Ravena met Terrance's gaze and held it. Pressure rose in some higher battle of wills than Liza didn't understand, thickening the air, heating her face.

Terrance broke the silence. "You know what we're here for," he said.

"So say it, *knife*," said Ravena.

"You say it first, *Lady*," said Terrance.

"I was his knife first, you know," said Ravena, still unmoving, still unblinking, and the sound between her words was her fingernails carving stress into the resin of her desktop. "I know you. I know the darkness inside you. The hunger. The hate."

More games. Ravena's low, purring tone crawled under Liza's skin and made her shiver, and she wanted to just scream to make it stop.

"He never lets it out," said Ravena in a near-whisper, "and he never will. He's afraid. But I would do that for you. I would create for you a sheath that lets you draw blood as you need, that lets you take the flesh you've earned with you to your bed. You could be mine, knife, and you could do what you were born to do instead of remaining *bound*."

Terrance laughed, a forced and awful sound. "You *serious*?" he choked. "You actually think I'd leave him? For *you*?"

A bad silence came.

It hurt. It pressed into Liza's ears, dimmed the lights, turned all that white a slightly sick yellow, until Terrance's defiance simply died like flowers with no water. "No," he managed, no more laughter, no more dares, but still, he held his ground.

"Name your favor," said Ravena, letting him keep his victory.

"Seishirou, right?" he blurted, crossing his arms and legs at once. "You damn well know we're here about Seishirou."

"I reasoned as much," said Ravena lightly. "After all, who could hand-pick the people I need with such precision other than Jonathan, my child?"

"So you did make him?" said Salome, leaning forward. "He's yours? Hot damn, that's a doozy."

"It is a 'doozy,' yes," said Ravena, "and a messy bit of family drama I'm surprised your precious Father never told you. I thought he liked sharing his little victories."

"He don't boast," growled Terrance. "You *know* he don't, and if you say one more thing about him—"

What was *wrong* with everybody? "Jonathan offered us a favor if we did this for you and retrieved Seishirou," Liza interrupted, and everyone stared at her. "What?" she said. "What's the point of playing these stupid games? We *know* who's strongest, we *know* whose house we're in, and we're all just wasting time comparing condom size!"

Ravena laughed again, and Liza's heart clenched for one second of worry she'd gone too far, but it seemed she hadn't yet. "A breath of fresh air!" said Ravena. "Goodness, I thought I was the only one in our family tree who broke patterns, who walked on their edges, yet here you are—a baby, yet challenging *all the right things*." She smiled, impossibly sincere, brilliant like the full moon emerging from clouds. "Thank you, you delightful child. Yes. Let's waste no more time." Ravena clapped her hands.

Three humans entered from the hall bearing dazed smiles and silver trays, their sleeves rolled up to their elbows to show neatly scarred forearms. On each tray sat a crystal tumbler and a knife.

"We're doing it properly now, of course," said Ravena, so friendly, so non-threatening, that all the tension and weirdness and formality seemed a bad dream. "Blood drawn and shared, promises made. That's how it should be done, anyway. I'm a little old-fashioned sometimes."

Liza wanted to go along with this sudden sweetness, but it had to be another game. The power was still in play. It had just changed.

Terrance eyed the humans. "They're not . . . they're not willing, are they?"

"Does it matter?" Ravena smiled again, mocking now—a repertoire of smiles like Liza never imagined one person could wield—and gestured. "Go on. Draw blood."

"This is more old-fashioned than *I* know about," said Salome, sitting higher to peer at the tray. "How's it work?"

"Oh, it's simple," said Ravena, and produced a scapel out of thin air. "We drink each other's blood, and we make an oath."

She slit her wrist.

It didn't bleed long. Her skin closed over the wound, leaving no sign of entry, but she'd expertly directed what spilled into a silver cup.

The scent of such powerful blood made Liza feel loopy.

"Maybe I oughta make *that* my next scent," muttered Salome.

"Pretty sure that'd go down like a lead balloon," said Terrance, but he followed suit. His blood spilled into his crystal goblet, and he took a full thirty seconds more to heal than Ravena.

Salome picked up her scalpel to do the same.

So did Liza. It was hard not to flinch.

Ravena licked her own forearm clean—a quick and simple movement that skewed Liza's perception. The burn from the cut helped, and she focused on it while it healed over the next minute.

"Feel free to refill your tanks," said Ravena, indicating the humans.

"I don't drink from the unwilling," said Terrance as though that needed to be said, as though that weren't one of the key rules.

"They aren't unwilling, knife. They weren't when they signed up, anyway, and they haven't complained yet, not even on their days off."

Salome gave Ravena a dry look and licked her own arm clean, too. "No, thanks." Somehow, she'd kept it from staining her dress.

Terrance had gotten his blood everywhere, a sanguine sort of protest.

Liza licked her blood off her arm. She hadn't done that since before she'd been made, and it tasted strange.

"As it happens, I am willing to make such a trade," said Ravena as she took each crystal receptacle and poured them together into her silver one. "That is because I am bored with him. Also, I do happen to need some help. How fortuitous." She sipped, then held it out. "I vow to treat you as my own family while you are here, and to deliver Seishirou to you once you have fulfilled your use to me."

Terrance snatched it so roughly that Liza was surprised it didn't spill. "That's vague as hell." He sipped. "I vow to do you *one* favor, one good one, in exchange for Seishirou's life." Then he hesitated. "You don't have to do this, by the way," he said to Liza softly. "We'll cover for you if you don't."

"No, I'm in. I promised," said Liza, and took a sip.

The addition of Ravena's blood socked her in the face like 120-proof rum, and she lost track of things for a moment. "I promise, uh. I'll do a favor." *Good thing I'm not driving right now,* she thought.

"Sure," said Salome, sipping and returning the silver cup. "One favor, in trade. Works for me. So whaddaya need, doll?" she said, since they were apparently all friends now.

Ravena placed the unfinished cup on her desk. "A three-part problem with a three-part solution. Tonight, I am holding a feast to indulge certain suitors of mine who believe that being female and human in appearance makes me susceptible to the flattery and fear to which our *honorable* Father is apparently immune. It must happen; civility dictates as much, wasteful as it all is. However, I have every reason to believe one of my suitors is trying to kill me."

They stared.

Ravena laced her fingers again. "There have been several pitiful attempts, of late—stupid things like sawdust in food, silver arrows, that sort of item. Obviously, someone is ill-informed and desperate, but I am tired of playing these little games."

Terrance leaned forward; all his aggression seemed to have transformed into focus. "And you're sure it's a so-called suitor?"

"I am. One of my children managed to inform me that someone would be here tonight to 'do it properly,' and then she was killed. I do not take that lightly."

That hit worse than any swallow of blood.

Family was everything—drilled, bound, and consummated. The murder of one was an insult to all, and this knowledge settled in her like lead-lined grief. "We got to tell Father," she said.

"Someone dared?" said Terrance, low. "Someone feckin' *dared* kill one of us?"

"Tell Father," said Liza again, slightly choked. "You have to tell Father, and then he can—"

"He can what, child?" Ravena said, softly. "I promise you, he already knows; yet he has promised *me* he will not interfere with my family, and I hold him to it. He's interfered enough. I will not invite him into this, as it would further erode the independence and authority I carved for myself through the granite of time."

"Oh," said Liza because she had to say something.

"So you want me to kill the killer?" said Terrance. "That my favor?"

"Obviously, but first, we must discover who he or she is," said Ravena. "And before we can do that, we need distraction—something you're talented at, my dear." This was to Salome.

Salome blinked. "You want me to dance?"

"If you would be so kind."

"Huh. That's easy," said Salome, pursing her lips. "The wind might join me, a little. Maybe I can have access to your lab and herb garden first."

"Of course."

Liza shifted. "What about me?"

Ravena smiled, showing no teeth, and Liza realized this was the most dangerous of her repertoire. "Tonight, my dear, you will be my date. This gives me some needed personal space and allows you to inspect all those who dare enter my presence."

Liza stared. "Well," she finally said. "It wouldn't the worst evening out I ever had."

Ravena laughed again as the humans shambled out, untasted.

CHAPTER 4

THE PARTY

Fifteen-year-old Liza would have loved next few hours. Grown-up Liza just wanted it to stop.

Ravena had acquired the use of the Gherkin for the evening, and that was nerve-wracking. Now that the dragon war in New Delhi had smashed centuries of magical secrecy, it wasn't unusual for a magical being with wealth to do something like this, but it still seemed a ballsy move for a night of assassination.

It was beautiful here, though. The dome rose overhead in muntin-crossed glory, exposing the whole sky, laying all of London out at their feet. Stars gleamed, magically revealed to compete with what city lights showed through the thick evening fog. Towers punctured it to rise like sparkling pillars holding up the night sky, emphasizing the feeling of being on an island, floating, above it all.

Beneath that dome strode some among the most powerful magical beings in all of creation.

Liza schooled her face, relaxed her body language, and followed like a ridiculously tall shadow as Ravena slid between those beings like fingers through sand.

Ravena had dressed Liza up in a heavy, beaded gown that swung and sparkled with every step like moonlight on black water. The shoes—if anything with a heel this high could still be called that—put her head and shoulders above nearly everyone here. Diamond combs dug into her skull, gleaming in the mass of her hair like galaxies, and Ravena's makeup artist had turned her face into something smoky, into something sexy, into the face of a rich stranger who maybe owned islands and bet on lives for fun.

Ravena outshone her completely.

When they had met, Ravena had taken steps to look *less* beautiful. She'd minimized her angles, downplayed her eyes, thinned her lips. Now, that was done, and Ravena aimed to burn.

She was a goddess in red, golden-dark and frightening, lightning in a night sky. Her black curls cascaded down her back, tempting and scented, and her eyes and her smile seemed utterly unreal, impossible, too perfect to be true.

What Liza envied, however, was her confidence.

The beings in this room represented half the known worlds and a good portion of the Seven Peoples. Liza spotted Fey, Darkness, and Sun; there were no humans or Guardians, very few Kin, and absolutely nobody who wasn't *somebody*. She recognized ministers and magisters and presidents and kings, only some of whom bothered with a presence on the Ever-Dying Earth. They ruled in their own parallel worlds and did not need this human habitation.

They'd still shown up for Ravena.

All of them wore enough wealth to fund the world's orphanages for a decade, and Liza struggled to see this *apart* from human finances, *apart* from the life she'd once lived, somehow above and beyond it.

She couldn't do it very well.

"Yes, thank you, it's lovely to see you, too," said Ravena, kissing the cheek of a passing character with fins for ears and blue skin. "This is my companion. Isn't she magnificent? No touching! This evening, *she is mine*."

Statements like that had been coming all night long, and they had an effect. Those Ravena told clearly began imagining possible activities for Ravena's evening with the woman at her back, and doing so focused their desire on Ravena, lamprey-like, with an almost hungry ferocity.

It hurt to watch. Ravena had power, had the might of night and strength and wind, and had certainly wielded it longer than anyone else in this room; yet the sidelong looks, the smirking glances, and supposedly seductive conversations reduced her to an object.

Liza could not understand why Ravena allowed it.

Bafflingly, these guests seemed to think they could bribe the Blood Queen with stupid gifts and baubles. They made offers of trade, exchanges of talented people, stock in business ventures.

The suitors were on another level.

There was Empress Mer'Qel, who ruled the oceans in multiple worlds and had brought a small contingent of gill-cheeked warriors with her. She'd united and held all the various underwater clans through war and rumored merciless strength, and had come prepared to woo tonight not with beauty, but with wealth. Her people all wore outfits made from long-forgotten silks and jewels, with treasures lost over millennia through the many seas of the many worlds. It was an unbelievable trove on display tonight; just the collar Mer'Quel wore was priceless, allowing her to breathe air as long as she wanted.

Her people were limited to bubbles of water around their heads like cosmonaut helmets, but everything couldn't be perfect.

Liza supposed the fact that Ravena didn't need to breathe might be a reason for this sought-after match, but it still didn't make sense. Ravena must have something Mer'Quel wanted, but what?

Perhaps the same thing Bran wanted. The newly enthroned Bran the Crow King, Bran the Conqueror, was among the most human-looking of the crowd tonight, but Liza was not fooled. He was Father's friend, and she'd met him. He looked nothing like a human, but he wore his disguise well—a pale and dark-haired rogue-pirate sort of thing, with an easy smile that was all his and a physique his tuxedo *really* loved. He nodded at her, raising a glass.

She nodded back. Bran ruled the entire realm of the Darkness, the entire parallel *world* of Umbra, and countless creatures of terrifying and wonderful mien. Why was Bran here? And why court *her*? Bran had no need for wealth, no need for power or soldiers. More than that, he was Father's friend, so surely—

"Hey," said Terrance quietly by Liza's shoulder.

"Funny, seeing you shorter'n me right now," said Liza.

"Yeah, real funny." Terrance wore all black, including vest and shirt, and his shoes were not shiny. Other than his violently orange-red hair, he might as well be wrapped in shadow. "How you holding up?" He spoke looking around, constantly scanning for threats.

Liza checked Ravena's proximity and the body-language of the parasites surrounding her. "Fine. I suppose."

"This place is full of wicked people," said Terrance casually. "And I am very wicked, so I know what I'm saying."

Liza wasn't about to argue. This wasn't a safe party. Jewels and fancy gowns meant nothing; this was not, not, *not* safe. "Have you seen Salome?"

"Not yet. She'll be up soon, I think." He nodded toward a small stage set up against the curve of the dome, tastefully spotlit. "When she moves, nobody'll look at anything else."

"Ravena *is* here," Liza reminded him.

"Trust me. This is a game I've played before, and that's how it'll work," said Terrance. "I'm hoping we can find the killer before she starts, or it'll be harder."

Liza frowned "Why?"

"Because that's when I'd do. Everybody enchanted and relaxed? Perfect time to stab a kidney."

Liza shook her head. "Glad to know you have the mind of a killer."

"I'm here to help," he lilted. "Keep your eyes out. There's nobody innocent here tonight."

Something about that phrase burned itself into her, branded her already stressed nerves. "Who's your favorite?"

Terrance shrugged. "Could be anybody. Take Baron Tem, the pale guy over yonder. He's a nasty character, poisoning his way to his position. He's rich, though; there's rumors he owns the moon."

Liza snorted.

Terrance was apparently serious. "That brickhouse fellow over there is Brenin Brenin, who claims he has himself a world rivaling the Silver Dawning. He's got some deal going with Umbra; they keep exchanging unique metals and jewels. Mer'Quel's collar was made by Brenin's people, so he may not be bluffing."

Liza shifted, staying close to Ravena as the other woman moved. "Is everybody here connected?"

"Better believe it. See them over there, the one with the octopus arms and no face? They claim to come from some faraway water world with sentient oceans, but all I know is they wield a magic no one can identify. They don't usually leave their cave, either. A proposal from them is *very* weird."

Liza almost rubbed her face, then stopped just in time to spare her makeup. "There's too much to keep track of."

"I know. Just keep your eyes on *her*. Keep her safe. I'll take down the baddie when they make their move." And he was gone.

Liza turned to do that and spotted a guest no one had talked about.

He looked like a tall black man, but strange instinct told her he was a member of the Dream. That was remarkable. Among the Seven Peoples of the Earth, the Dream had, to put it frankly, *noped out* generations before, opting to hide in some kind of in-between realm that bore no definition and held no life apart from the Dream themselves, who were all asleep until the end of time. Or so went the lore.

The few members of the Dream who'd stayed in the human world were aloof, strange, hard to contact, and apparently lived by feeding on things like dreams and the consciousness of coma patients.

Liza turned to check on Ravena, turned back, and couldn't remember what she'd been doing.

Coma patients. Weird. Why had she been thinking that?

Ravena moved a couple of feet from her, and she hurried to catch up. There was something she'd forgotten, though. Something . . .

"This is Liza. She's mine for the night. Tomorrow, her dance card will be open again—depending on how well she recovers, of course," Ravena purred, and the thing with four heads talking to her burbled a wet, tar-like laugh.

Liza sighed. Her feet hurt. It took a *lot* for a Night-Child's feet to hurt.

"Gazpacho?" offered a passing kobold.

She waved him off.

Clusters of dangerous beings chuckled and talked, making nice, pretending to be friends, ignoring the tension that lay like uncomfortable damp sheets between people and skin. How much longer could this go on? And what had she forgotten?

"You should be careful," whispered someone right in her ear. "It's happening soon."

Liza spun to find no one there.

"Oh, good," she said to no one. "I'm being haunted. That's all I need."

Some weirdo was trying to get Ravena to give them a lock of her hair in exchange for a condo in Majorca. Ravena put them off, smiling, laughing, flirting just enough, and then a rare, brief pause came when nobody was grabbing at her and nobody was talking to her.

Liza was bored enough to lean in and take another risk. "I have a question," she said, bent down so her lips were near the other woman's ear. "Do you actually enjoy this?"

Ravena's perfect smile did not change. "No."

"Then how the bloody hell are you managing without snapping everybody's necks?"

Ravena touched her lips to Liza's cheek and murmured against her skin. "I hate them all. Hate births power. It's not new hate, which is like lava, angry and uncontrollable. It's old, older than they are, and so instead, it hardens around my heart." She shifted, her lips moving to Liza's ear. "None of these pieces of dog feces can get to me. But if I let them think they can, they'll keep trying, and as long as that occupies them, I'll always know where they are."

Liza hadn't expected a real answer. She stared.

"You're doing so well, child." Ravena went back to the wolves.

The hour neared midnight, and most of the Fey had gone to bed.

Morning people, all of them, and while their absence hadn't really made a dent, the party as a whole seemed much less shiny, somehow, and distinctly more ominous.

Liza had managed not to mentally check out, but it was close. As far as she could tell, nobody needed her here.

Jonathan had asked her to come, had made extra eye-contact and done everything but beg. But what was the purpose? Terrance would do the deed, and in a moment, Salome would show up and blow everybody's minds.

Surely Liza wasn't here just to be decoration. Surely not.

Tired, bristly, she began to grind her teeth as she shadowed Ravena. *She. Was not. Decoration.*

She couldn't dismiss the thought once it appeared, but there seemed nothing to do except let it fill her skull. Walking away would cause more problems than there already were, but that rising, irritated voice inside her was flavored by the always-wrath of her Beast, by her very young and insistent hunger, and had no outlet.

A man stepped in front of her.

Liza found herself facing that member of the Dream again (that's what she'd forgotten!), a black man, handsome and bearded and as tall as she was.

She knew him.

But she didn't know him. At once, dizzyingly, she knew and *did not know this man*, and she stiffened, swaying in her heels.

He steadied her. "'I will wear my heart upon my sleeve for daws to peck at; I am not what I am,'" he said.

Liza blinked. "What?"

"Shakespeare," said the man, who was handsome in a way she couldn't define, features simple yet perfect, his salt-and-pepper beard trimmed and his accent comfortably familiar.

"What are you blabbering about?" she said.

"Not everyone here is what they seem, and yet some are truer than true," said the man, and it was nonsense, fortune-cookie gibberish, yet it poured down her spine like ice cubes and warning.

Liza glanced away to see if Terrance was near.

Wait. Why was she looking for him?

She'd forgotten something.

That's right—*she was not a decoration.* This was a frustrating assignment, beneath any woman, and she—

The man tapped her shoulder, she turned, remembered him.

The world tilted, train shaking as if to pull itself apart.

"What did you do to me?" she said softly.

"It isn't your fault," said the man. "I am of the Dream, and your waking mind cannot hold me. My name is Jackal."

He hadn't said *Jackal.* He said something else, some weird and ancient word invoking desert nights and pack hunters and canine faces on human bodies, but she couldn't parse that word and had to accept what her brain delivered in its place. "Okay," she said slowly. "So before I forget you again—which is creepy as hell, by the way—what do you want?"

The party dimmed. Sounds faded; colors lost life, movement grew sleepy and still as the people around her slowed like hardening cement.

Her heart beat in pain, a strange, sideways shudder.

"I have taken you out of time for one moment only," said Jackal. "Listen well. You, Elizabeth Oshun Thomas Night, have been chosen for a crossroad."

She couldn't breathe. Could barely exhale to speak. "I don't understand."

"You will be given a choice the moment you look away from me again," said Jackal. "This choice carries a cost: either you save her, and in doing so put her on a path where she may drag your Father down to death, or you let her be killed, allow it, and in doing so, put your Father on a path to yet longer life."

Did blinking count as looking away? She didn't dare test it. "How is that even a choice?"

"You will not have time to think through it."

"Are you having a laugh at me right now?"

"I don't have a sense of humor," said Jackal, though she suspected that dry delivery might *be* his humor.

"Can . . . can you give me more detail than that?"

"No. But when you make this choice, it will have great personal cost, for you will either have chosen to keep your blood oath or break it."

Liza took shallow, quick breaths, unable to dismiss him, unwilling to look away. She was clutched, pincered, trapped. This wasn't a joke. "Why are you telling me this? Did Jonathan send you?"

"Jonathan does not yet know me," said Jackal.

She tried to disbelieve him and found she could not. Instead, she grew angry.

"Bull," she said.

"Oh?" said Jackal, so politely.

"I'm not responsible for what anyone chooses to do with their days," said Liza. "Do you hear me? No one is responsible for anybody else. Nobody *makes* you kill somebody, or *makes* you steal, or *makes* you pull any amount of bloody nonsense. What you're saying is garbage. My choice, responsible for what Ravena does? Bull."

"What will you do then with the information I've given you?" said Jackal with a weird, infuriating boredom as if he knew she'd say those things, knew what decision she'd make, and it only made her angrier.

"It's none of your business what I'll do with it," she said. "I'll make the choice I have to make, whatever that is, and you'll find out the same time as everyone else."

"Good," he said, and just like that, the world resumed noise, color, movement. Just like that, Jackal was gone. Just like that, the moment came.

Liza was facing *away* from Ravena for some unremembered reason, facing the opposite end of the room, and that's why she saw it coming.

A gargoyle had leaped over the heads of the crowd with such speed and silent grace that almost nobody had noticed, and there was no time to think. No time to weigh pros and cons. It was already there, in mid-leap, arcing with terrifying ponderous weight right for her. No, not for her. For Ravena.

Ravena, who wasn't *nice*, but could be honest. Ravena, who could be murderous, and manipulative and dangerous and possibly insane—Ravena, who had lived nearly as many centuries as Notte, who knew so many things, who'd adapted to survive in a climate that never was and maybe never would be kind to her.

Ravena, who was a wicked and glorious treasure of life and will. For her to die like this would dent the world, leave a scar, gouge a hole that could never be filled.

Besides, Liza had promised.

She leaped to meet the monster in the air, and it *was* a monster, a hideous, beaked statue of a thing, clawed and fanged and terrifyingly pupil-free, and she intercepted with the wonderful new strength of the Blood, and she gloried in the way her body just *did what she told it to do*, and she crashed into it with every ounce of will she possessed.

They collided.

Bones broke. It crushed her arms. Its rough stone beak snapped an inch from her face.

Her Beast came out to play.

Liza could never say why, later. Maybe it was the raw weight of the creature as she interrupted its leap, or maybe it was the warmth pulsing through its stone carapace that told her it had a heart and it had blood and was very much alive, or maybe in her pain, she just lost control.

Maybe it was because the gargoyle's blood smelled like fresh-cut stone and power.

Mine, her Beast thrilled at the creature, and with a jaw strength she'd never have imagined if she were sane, she bit the gargoyle's throat to rubble.

CHAPTER 5

A GOOD OFFENSE

t turned out gargoyles had blood. A *lot* of it.

It didn't taste good, but it was strangely pleasing, settling, like the bitter dark chocolate she used to enjoy in the evenings years ago. Liza forgot that people were watching, forgot Ravena and Terrance and everyone else, and simply latched on like a tick, taking her fill.

The monster beat at her, pounded with fists to turn flesh to jelly and bones to dust, but the Beast did not give a fuck about pain, and she healed too fast for it to force her away. When they'd crashed together to the ground, pieces of its body cracked off as she began to smash it back, and she didn't stop. She clawed into its crumbling abdomen, snapped off its flailing arms, and kept drinking, drinking, drinking.

It took a while.

When Liza finally came to herself, slow awareness of a crowd and public scrutiny wriggled into her belly and under her skin with hot, weird embarrassment. She was covered in gray blood and panting, her sex warm. The monster's body was rubble, pieces of it spread all around the room and crunching underfoot.

The guests murmured quietly, standing in a circle around her. It seemed they hadn't decided if this was entertainment or trouble.

She sat up, straddling it, and found she wasn't alone.

Terrance sat on the floor beside her, waiting. "Hey," he said, as if gargoyle death was a daily event.

"Hey," she said back, and licked gray, glistening gore from her lips.

"Got a little something there." He handed her a handkerchief.

"This thing tried to kill Ravena," said Liza, and she said it loudly, because it was true.

"Yeah, we figured that out," said Terrance. "Are you all right?"

He meant *Are you back in control?*

He meant *I thought we lost you there.*

He meant *Please be okay or I will have to kill you because that's my job.*

Her heart skipped a beat, but she nodded. "I'm fine." She offered the gluey handkerchief back, which he declined. "I promise. I'm good." One of her diamond combs hung painfully from her Afro, and she yanked it free.

"Glad to hear it," said Terrance. "All clear!" He stood, and servants came out of the shadows, kobolds and goblins and things she did not know, to begin the process of cleaning up dead gargoyle.

"Well, wasn't that entertaining?" Ravena called cheerfully as if there weren't smeared vampire in the middle of the floor. "I do apologize, everyone. Territory disputes in New South Wales should produce opals, not effluvium, but I suppose there's no accounting for taste."

Her audience tittered politely.

Still straddling the gargoyle, Liza twisted to stare at her, half in awe, half horrified.

Ravena smiled as though someone had merely spilled a drink. "The floor show—if you'll pardon my humor—is over now. Would you follow me, please? I have just the thing to get this taste out of all our mouths. Come along. Watch your shoes!"

Someone laughed, a little more genuinely. The murmuring rose, approaching normal volume. And they obeyed her, stepping around the rubble, avoiding puddles of gray blood, following her lead and parting around Liza as though she and her prey were a rock in a stream.

"Gotta be kidding me," she whispered.

"Get used to it," said Terrance. "Human world, there'd be police and people with masks and gloves all over the place, but among the Mythos? Not so much. Everybody saw what happened. This guy was dead the second you got your teeth in him. So what's left to do? Nothing but get back to hedonism."

Liza looked around again. Something was missing—something she couldn't remember. She shook her head. "So the show's over and that's it. Are we done?"

"Don't think so." Terrance stood and offered her his hand. "Somebody killed Ravena's child—not smart, and put her on guard. Somebody *also* got sawdust into her food, which is deadly to her, for all she made fun. This guy don't strike me as the clever type."

Liza stood, wobbly. She'd broken one of the heels, and bent to undo the straps. "Hell," she summarized.

"Pretty much. Come on, love. Here's something to enjoy: you won't find many occasions when the doers and movers in the world see you for what you truly are. Enjoy it while it lasts."

"Blending in isn't an option now, anyway," said Liza, taking stock. The gray blood somehow didn't show on her dress. It merely marked her skin, silver on brown, making her feel like some kind of hunting goddess.

The blood really agreed with her system. It wasn't human—she couldn't live on it—but it settled in like stone strength, like weightiness that could crack tile with every step.

She joined the crowd, head held high, no longer shadow or decoration but devil. She knew they'd part for her, pretending they weren't moving the hell out of her way, but she knew they were, and *they* knew they were, and Liza couldn't stop making them, wandering, roaming, forcing world leaders to slide around her like magnets of opposing force.

Power. This was power. Maybe fear, maybe respect, but definitely power. So this was a taste of how it would feel when she grew older, centuries in to life as a Night-Child, and accumulated strength of her own. It tasted good.

At long last, Salome appeared on the stage.

She came from nowhere and stood barefoot under the lights, swaying before the music even started. Her face hidden by her hair, alternately shadowed and gleaming, she moved as though casting spells with her whole body.

It was something in her smile, or maybe her elfin form; she gave the impression that gravity was only a consideration. An indefinable scent came with her, a cloud of subtle sweetness, a wish of wisteria and summer breezes, and it brought flushes to cheeks and happiness to mind. When the music finally began, piped in from somewhere else and apparently live, it seemed she'd conjured it from her heart.

It was impossible to watch Salome dance and not be changed.

Her hair flew around her face like a veil and up like a wild dark crown, and her shift pressed against her body to reveal hints of what lay beneath but never enough to distract. Her feet never missed; her heels rarely touched. She spun around couples and turned them toward her with light in their eyes; she surrounded single dancers until they twisted in her wake like wind-strewn petals. She kissed the cheeks of furiously blushing monsters and ran her fingers through their hair as she passed, touching lips, necks, ears with the briefest caress, and as she did, the scent lingered, until it seemed they were far from the city, standing someplace magical and verdant. She spun, and her tassel skirt flew out like to shine like strands of diamonds, then wrapped around her legs like an embrace

Soon, the room's occupants all moved with her, swaying or softly humming, as though caught in a spell she wove simply by being alive. She moved with the music like a leaf caught in current. Had she been human, she would have sweated, flagged, tired. She was not human, and so she simply danced.

Salome danced, and the world had no choice but to fall in love.

Damn it, there *was* something Liza had forgotten.

She couldn't find it, couldn't dig it out, and that was more than strange; she didn't just forget things, and maybe it wasn't important, but her instinct said it was. It was like waking up to the loss of an arm or a leg and finding the balance one knew was lost and broken and had to be relearned.

Somehow, though it hurt, Liza turned away from Salome, trying to regain that balance, trying to find what she'd forgotten, and that's when she saw him.

Bran was moving steadily toward Ravena through the crowd.

It was a slow pace, utterly smooth and unintrusive. He bumped no one, disturbed no one's view. Something dark like smoke rose around him in sentient wisps, obscuring attention, diverting view. His own gaze was locked on the back of Ravena's head, and the look on his face was murder.

Him? thought Liza, baffled, briefly undone.

But he was coming.

She moved, shoved people out of the way with gargoyle strength to stand between, leaving a swath of growling people in her wake.

Bran stopped.

The crowd murmured because Salome had gone still. The music, wherever it came from, stumbled to a halt mid-transition, leaving a terrible sense of incompletion, a heavy and nauseating silence.

"Damn," said Terrance from beside her, though when he'd gotten there, she did not know. "You, man? You? Don't do this."

Bran knew better, *had to know better*, because to attack any of Father's family was to make an enemy of Father himself. Bran was Father's friend. He knew.

"Well, well, well," said Ravena, almost to herself.

Bran's impressive jawline tightened. His eyes blazed with a horrible anger, with the kind of wrath that could spill onto innocent people. "Hello, Ravena. We haven't spoken tonight."

"Don't do it, man," Terrance said again. His knives were out, one in each hand. "This won't end well."

"I have reasons," said Bran, and he bared perfect white teeth in a snarl that threatened to smash all civility to bits. "I don't want to fight you, *knife*, but I will if I have to. Move."

"No," said Terrance, and grief darkened his tone. "I got a job tonight. It's up to you if you're making that job into you."

The tension was heart-bursting, flame-broiling, skin melting bad, and nobody seemed to care. Liza clenched her fists, preparing to fight.

Who was she kidding? This was the Crow King, lord of Umbra, undisputed ruler of the Darkness.

If they fought, she was going to die.

Jonathan promised, she thought, and wondered why she'd believed him so easily.

"I tire of this evening," said Ravena, and her voice was steel, and her voice was ice, and she raised that voice like an executioner's axe and brought it down on what was left of the party's throat. "This is the second attempt on my life tonight, and I find myself insulted."

No one moved.

Mer'Quel suddenly spat on the floor with more volume than moisture. "This is how the royalty treats its hosts on land? Pathetic. Queen of Blood, I will see you again. We go now."

"That is a good idea, dear. In fact, you should *all* go. Now." Ravena's power rose with her visible anger, pushing in waves, separating clusters, spurning them toward the door.

Then came an awkward few moments while everyone not involved in murder-time left and chatted and grabbed last-minute snacks from the hors d'oeuvre trays.

"Now, *this* is how you do it," muttered a hairy fellow with six eyes and a dark purple tux as he passed.

"I know, right?" said his companion, whose horse-like face hinted at interesting ancestry. "Intrigue and murder! I like that."

"Too right, you are," said the other, and then they were out of range.

One by one, the extras exited via elevators, the stairs, or simple magic, until finally Ravena and those who orbited her like planets were left in terrible silence.

Bran, Terrance, Salome, and Liza stood where they were, pillars in some passion play only one of them understood.

"They're his, not yours," said Bran evenly. "How did you get them to fend for you?"

"I have my ways," said Ravena sweetly. "Bran, *dear* Bran, are my little cousins here correct? Do you truly mean to do me, faithful denizen of your realm, harm?"

"Yes," said Bran, and then he moved.

Liza never had a chance. The gargoyle may have given her strength, raw mass and inertia propelled by will, but this was *speed*, this was magic, this was power on a level she did not understand, and she found herself knocked aside so hard and so fast that when she came to on a the floor a moment later, she briefly didn't know where she was.

Terrance had stopped him, but not by much.

They stood locked in blade challenge, muscles strained, teeth bared. Neither could move; the knives trembled, and Bran's blades hissed like angry snakes. Bran was snarling, making a horrible nightmare-noise at odds with his human guise. Terrance's shoes had left grooves in the floor, and a bit of exposed wiring sparked between them.

Ravena sounded so bored. "Really, this is beneath you."

"Only the dead are beneath death," growled Bran, and exploded out of his human costume into his true form, tall, brick-red, covered in cracks that flickered as if his heart burned miles away. Black horns gleamed like polished ebony, and he bared a mouth full of fangs and roared.

Fists, knives, power flew, and Liza couldn't follow it. Sounds and sparks and rubble skittered over the floor or smacked into the glass, and suddenly Terrance and Bran were locked again, inches from Ravena, and Terrance was bleeding everywhere, just everywhere.

But he held his ground. His shoes had exploded; bare feet braced, bloodied knuckles gripping both blades, he smiled. "Oh, you *are* fun," he said as though he weren't visibly trembling with strain. "We should'a sparred before now. Maybe next time you come for dinner?"

But Bran was not going there, not calming down, *not smiling back*, and he spoke now with the echoing far-away words of warning and doom. "I will destroy you, knife, if I must. Her life belongs to me, and that of her own doing."

Ravena sighed. "Bran, *really*. I don't even know what this is about."

And Bran gawked at her, staring over Terrance's head, the baffled look almost funny in spite of his terrifying form.

Ravena tapped her chin. "Two points. One, I'm not certain I want to explain to you-know-who why we killed his knife tonight, are you? Two, I feel I ought to remind you that I know you're coming now. Dear, you've lost the element of surprise, *and that means you've lost.*"

Bran roared at her, and the force of it pushed Liza to the floor again.

Ravena roared back. Bared her fangs, opened her eyes wide so their sudden glow blazed to fill the room. Wind came from nowhere, gripping them, unreasonably cold and promising strange and painful things. Bran slid back an inch, struggling, keeping his place by stubbornness and wrath.

Liza stayed on the floor, trembling. Salome leaped off the stage. Terrance didn't move, though a flush had climbed his pale cheeks, hiding his freckles.

The wind died. The glow in Ravena's eyes faded. She smiled sweetly. "Shall we talk this out like civilized monsters?"

Bran hesitated for a too-long moment, then nodded at Terrance. Simultaneously, they disengaged.

Bran's blades were scored, notched, near-destroyed, and hissing smoke. "Shame," he said, looking at them. "I liked these. There's wood in the center, you see, so it would have at the very least hurt like a bitch."

Terrance did not put his own notched blades away, but stood still, refusing to look away even when Ravena trailed her fingertips along the back of his neck.

"This seems personal," she said. "Why did you do this?"

"You know why," threatened Bran.

"No. I don't. I never would have let you pretend to court me if I did."

Bran pointed one ruined blade at her, its missing tip who knew where. "Joshua Run. Katie Lin."

Ravena began to look confused. It didn't seem a familiar expression, and twisted uncomfortably on her brow. "What about them?"

Bran's growl was back, and Liza could feel it in the floor. "You took Joshua."

"I am allowed to make whomever I please into one of my children."

"He was not willing!" snarled Bran. "And I don't care that you do things differently than Notte—you had no right!"

"He angered me," said Ravena. "I had every right."

"You did not. He was my friend."

She scoffed. "Your *friend*? He was human! And I suppose the Lost Lin is what, your fiancé?" Bran bared his fangs, and Ravena bared hers back. "Don't lie to me. She's a mongrel, and she actually embraces it. What is this really about?"

Bran's roar cracked the glass, and panes fell shattering to the floor, spraying glass, leaving gaping maws that sucked night air into the dome.

"My goodness," said Ravena.

"You tried to murder her!"

"I did not," said Ravena. "She is quite alive, last I checked."

"You harmed her! You harassed her! You threatened her family!" said Bran, pointing again. "She does not have the power to stand up to you, but *I do*, and I claim the right to your life!" He took a step, crunching broke glass beneath his shiny black hooves *"I will have your life before you have hers!"*

Ravena's confusion had gone to disgust, a bafflement that tasted bad. "Why?"

"*Why?*" roared Bran, and more glass fell as he took another step.

"No closer, friend," warned Terrance, who had not given ground.

"Yes. Why?" said Ravena, actually recoiling, pulling back as though *this* behavior, not the threats but the choice of companions, left her repulsed.

"They're my *friends*!" Bran trumpeted.

Ravena shook her head. "I don't understand you, but it seems you are sincere," she said as though she couldn't believe the words coming out of her mouth. "So for the sake of respect, I will take this seriously. You cannot have my life until I am paid what I am owed."

"What *you* are owed?" he snarled.

"I no longer *have* Joshua Run. He's my child, but your precious Notte took him from me, so you'll have to pay the price for that loss, first. Then, there is the question of the Lost Lin."

"*What about her*?" he bellowed.

"She cost me. Her interference wrecked a plan I'd been working on for the past fifty years."

"With my grandfather, who is now *dead* because of that plan!" said Bran.

"You're welcome."

"Easy, there," said Terrance. "Everyone take it easy. Take a breath. There has to be a way to do this without starting a war, eh?"

Bran hissed, anger quickening his breath, and then he did a terrible thing: he smiled. It was a Cheshire smile, a cruel smile, a one-move-from-checkmate smile, and Liza thought, *Oh, no.* "I have a solution," he said. Darkness swirled around him, obscuring him in a crawling, climbing smoke that vanished almost at once, wrapping him in his human disguise once more. A foot shorter, smiling and sharp-jawed, he looked like he hadn't just been fighting and slicing and snarling. "Marry me."

Oh, NO, thought Liza, because the trap was obvious, the lure, the red blanket waved before the bull.

"What?" said Ravena in a low voice.

"You will marry me for real," Bran rumbled. "No more games. Our kingdoms will officially be one, and your people will be mine. *You* will be mine."

"*You dare?*" Ravena snarled, her fists clenched.

"I know you, Blood Queen, empress of your own fucking domain. Know what else I know? Once we wed, it won't matter what power you have. You'd be the Crow King's wife, now and forever, and you can't even be the mother of future heirs. From then on, *that* would be your name, your title, your status, and even if you murdered me in my sleep, you'd just be *that woman who killed the Crow King.* You want payment before I get what I'm owed? Surely *my* hand is a worthy prize. So I demand yours in payment."

With every ounce of effort she had left, Liza stood, forcing herself upright before it was too late.

Ravena took one step that sent a shockwave out from her to shatter more glass, one terrible, heavy step of pride and consequence and ancient Beast rage, of the weight of centuries fighting for *Ravena of Monmouth* and not *Notte's Oldest Child*, ready to avalanche toward Bran like a city sliding into the sea.

Liza stepped between them.

She couldn't say what made her do it. She had no place in this, no voice to use, no power or anything to leverage, but she moved because she knew what to do even though she felt insane. "Oy!" she said.

Everyone looked at her as if they didn't even know what she was.

The words just *came*. "Who protects your people if one of you dies?"

It was a simple question, one that ought not matter, and yet it seemed to land on Bran like a judge's gavel. He took a step back, staring at her as if slapped.

Ravena scowled. "Your precious Father would take everyone in, I've no doubt."

"And?" Liza challenged her. "You've made it very clear you think he does it all wrong, and now you're saying you'd just toss your entire line to him without caring? Just throw everything you've done down the crapper so you can be *right* in this one moment?"

It shouldn't have done anything, shouldn't have had an effect, but Ravena, too, took a step back, staring at her.

Inertia pulled, the train off the tracks and crashing through the fields. Liza turned to Bran again. "I know you're friends with Father. He calls *very few people* friends. You had to damn well earn that title, and you're going to throw it away for this? Because it would trash it all, and you know it. He's got principle, Bran. Even if he agreed with what you're doing, this would be attacking his family, and you'd lose. You'd lose his friendship, maybe your life, for sure lose people under you because *he would come for you*. Is that what you want? Is it?"

"I don't . . . ." Bran didn't continue.

Liza turned to Ravena. "You say you don't want Father involved. Bran may not be family, but you know how Father responds to his friends being attacked—and the way this looks right now, he'd assume you started something, especially after New Delhi. He would get involved."

Ravena paled, a strange look that was more lightning than midnight sky, yet she did not move.

Everyone was listening. Liza didn't dare consider her mental footwork lest she trip it up. "You're both right that there has been damage done," she said evenly. "It needs to be resolved, but not like this. Take some time." She breathed in, out, let the words sink in. "Take some time, calm down, and talk it out with a mediator. This isn't worth blowing up both your lives and everything you've worked so hard to build." Then she held her breath and waited.

No one moved.

They'd listened, though she hadn't presented a solution. They'd listened, though she had no right to speak. They'd listened, held still as though she now wielded the power to make people kneel at her feet.

"How long?" said Bran suddenly. "How long are we supposed to wait?"

"Oh, you young thing," said Ravena softly. Her Beast had tucked itself away, hidden once more, though Liza would never forget she'd seen it. "Is a week too long, little bird?"

Bran smiled like a hyena. "No. One week is just fine. Then we sit and hash this out, and I will have my justice."

"And will I have mine, too? I was *robbed*," Ravena said.

Bran hissed through his teeth. "We'll see. Maybe Liza here should be our mediator."

He'd said it in jest, but the moment he did, it became real.

Liza gulped audibly, a thing she hadn't known people could do outside of cartoons.

Ravena laughed lightly. "Yes, I think that will work very well."

Liza did not cry, *Hold on a damn minute!* The inertia was too strong. "Fine. But I'll probably bring backup."

"Not your Father," said Ravena. "He isn't allowed."

"No, someone else. I'll figure it out," said Liza.

"I'll come," said Terrance. "Been witness to most of this."

"You're biased, knife," said Ravena.

He turned and looked her in the eye. "If I were, you'd be dead, Lady."

She conceded the point with a slight bow of her head.

"One week," said Bran, low, focused like drawn bowstring. "And if you do not come, or if you refuse to make reparations, I will descend with all my world like a storm, and *we will devour* you. I will end your family line, and damn all the consequences to hell."

Liza shivered, fear sneaking into the cracks of her armor, but that wasn't Ravena's response. For the first time since all this started, the first time in the party, the first time all night, Ravena looked at Bran with heat, and her voice went low and husky. "Well," she said. "That might be fun."

Terrance went red again.

Bran may have been affected, but he hid it better. "One week. Where?"

"Here," said Ravena.

"Fine. One week. We will have until midnight. Prepare yourself." And black smoke again swirled around him like a barber pole from hell, and when it cleared, he was gone.

"What a silly way to have the last word," said Ravena, finally stepping down to the floor.

Terrance exhaled, slumping like a deflating balloon. "Well, that was a cock-up."

Liza wanted to go home so badly. She wanted to sleep for a week. No, she wanted to bathe in boiling water, *then* sleep for a week.

"As far as I'm concerned, you fulfilled your bargains with me," said Ravena. "In fact, I think I owe you all a little more than Seishirou's life—but for tonight, I'll thank you to take him and leave. I have damage control to do." She waved a hand at the whole ruined room.

"No kidding?" Terrance deadpanned.

"I have wizards on retainer for this sort of thing," she said. "They'll manage."

"Hey," said Salome, who'd straddled the dead gargoyle while no one was looking. She'd dipped her fingers in the blood and touched it to her tongue, staining her mouth. "This tastes like candy and arsenic. Can I have him?"

Ravena laughed.

Liza shook her head. After the evening's events, even that request seemed hardly worth the effort of pondering.

CHAPTER 6

SECRETS

Going home was not on the docket just yet.

Stained with gargoyle blood, she walked beside Ravena, expensive and hopelessly ruined shoes dangling from one hand. Terrance and the weird perverted kid from what felt like days before had gone to get Seishirou, which Ravena warned was not for the faint of heart.

Salome had gone with him out of curiosity.

Liza stayed behind.

She'd saved Ravena's life, rather a lot. She'd avenged the death of a sister she did not know, kept her word, and opened a can of worms that nauseated her just to think about. The meeting in a week was going to be hell. There were a lot of terrible things in Ravena's shadow, trailing like bad dreams, yet Liza could not abandon the idea that killing her would be wrong.

And whatever she'd forgotten was never coming back, either. *I'm losing it*, she thought.

"They won't take long," said Ravena, walking slowly. "I ordered Seishirou fed enough to heal. He'll be able to leave with you, though I have no idea if his mind is still intact." She shrugged.

Maybe, Liza thought, *I'm still too human. That, or everybody in the world sucks.*

"That was an impressive bit of magic earlier," said Ravena.

It took a moment to realize Ravena was talking to her. "What?"

And Ravena smiled, a sidelong, secret grin that carried experience and a frustrating tease of things Liza did not know. "Did your Father not tell you?" she said. "I suppose he hides things like this. Typical."

"Things like what?" Liza said slowly, unwillingly, unready for yet more things to wreck her worldview tonight, yet more secrets to slice through the comfort of facts.

Ravena turned that smile on her fully. "We're Kin, my sweet thing."

Liza shook her head. Did she mean Jonathan? "No, we're Night-Children. We started out Ever-Dying, and now we're of the Darkness."

"Don't quote the party line to me. I helped write it," said Ravena. "Listen to me, woman, and *think*. Your power is young, but if you don't learn to control it, you will harm someone you care about."

Okay, that was unexpected. Liza stared.

Ravena touched her cheek. "I will say this only once. *We are Kin*. We are not born magic like all the witches and wizards, like all the mixed-human races who can do wonderful things. You are correct: we were magicless, the Ever-Dying, but now we are not. We are those who *become Kin*—artificial Kin, artificial magic users, *created magic users*, and that is why the world fears us."

"I don't . . . " It hurt. Too many new things, too much to carry. Liza wanted to cry.

"Dear, we talk to the wind," said Ravena with a frustrating patience,

"That isn't . . . that's just a . . . "

"Each of us connected by *his* blood have unique power, and there is no way to predict what it will be. It isn't like ordinary Kin magic, diffuse and largely useless. We need no focal point, no wand. No herbs, no charms. *We are magic*, because we have been transformed, and singular, and can be more powerful than any natural-born Kin could be because *it only gets stronger over time*."

Liza stayed silent.

She considered facets, turning angles this way and that, and knew it was true. It went against everything she was taught. It was still true.

And it was dangerous. The other members of the Mythos already considered vampires freaks, able to transform the non-magical into something more, but what Ravena said went beyond that. It even went beyond Jonathan. "Magic can be artificially given to humans," Liza said, following the logical path.

Ravena smiled like the moon rising. "Yes."

"If the Mythos knew that, knew that something in us could empower *seven billion effing humans—*"

"You clearly have some kind of persuasion as your gift," said Ravena, skipping topics to let Liza wrestle that one on her own. "It's effective. You swayed *me*, sweetness, and not even your illustrious Father can do that."

Liza felt her throat close.

"Think about what I've said. Stay quiet. If Night didn't feel like telling you, then I'm sure he has his *reasons* for keeping you in the dark," said Ravena airily, breezily, cheerfully, and Liza got another taste of that deep and resounding hatred, that anger that went beyond a simple slight and into the realm of pure philosophical opposal, and couldn't think of anything to say.

Fortunately, that was when Terrance reappeared, half-carrying a naked, trembling, Japanese man.

Seishirou looked suspiciously whole. He'd healed—at least outwardly—from whatever had done to him, and left no sign he'd been flayed open, ripped apart and pinned with wooden stakes. He hung off Terrance's shoulders, expression that of a man who had no idea where he was, and did not speak.

Terrance's own expression was urgency. "Let's scram," said Terrance. "He ain't got much left of his mind in this condition."

"Oh, there's lots of wood in him still," said Ravena. "Just FYI."

Terrance curled his lip at her, but hid it quickly. "Yeah, thanks for that. Have a good life." He strode toward the door.

The kid who'd gone with him got there first and smiled as though this were all very funny. "He's quite the prize, eh?" he said.

"Shut it," said Terrance, hugged Seishirou close, and somehow went to dust with his burden.

Traveling with another person that way wasn't a trick Liza knew yet, but she promised herself she'd learn it.

"Know this," said Ravena softly. "I pay my debts."

"Was that a threat or a promise?" slipped out before Liza could stop it.

"Come on, little bat," said Salome, and looped her arm through Liza's. "Can't say it's been the perfect evening, but it wasn't boring, either. Later, doll." She dragged Liza through the door, ignoring the kid's leer.

Liza didn't look back. She knew Ravena was watching her, had told her things she wasn't supposed to know, had given her nuggets of truth she hadn't *owed* all evening long, and did not know what to make of it.

She could not shake the feeling that something big had happened here, a switch-change that put the whole world on a different track to somewhere unexpected.

This runaway train was never returning to station.

"Damn, I need a bath," Liza said.

"Yep," Salome agreed cheerfully, held her close, then pulled her into dust and took her home.

NOTTE'S BOOK OF KNOWLEDGE

In the time before time, the First War ended the peace of the Peoples of the Earth. Driven and desperate, survivors bred for power and magic, and they succeeded—with a legacy too great for their mortal forms, and a homeworld they left in pieces.

Afraid, they turned to Naktam, the Lord of Night Whispers, oldest of them all, and begged for advice—for he was strangest, and the most resilient. He knew Death by name, and embodied the hunger of all worlds; thus it was he taught them to define by families, to use soul's desire and blood's prime powerto join those like themselves.

The Seven Peoples of the Earth—the Sun, the Darkness, the Guardians, the Fey, the Dream, the Kin, and the Ever-Dying who have no magic—came to find their own through blood and spirit, and choose the symbols to rally by. In time, simpler symbols were added for the sake of time and varying skill.

Today, the Seven Peoples remain strong, balanced, and free, and few there are who fight this many-reined yoke.

THE SUN

Hunger: Hhealing.

Prime power: Light and heat.

Homeworld: Zenith, which is very hot, has numerous major stars, and is clean, regimented, and always welcomes those who are sick and require succor.

The People of the Sun bred for fire, light, qne heat, as a means to burn away infection and evil. This power grows over time; toward the end of their natural lifespan, their physical forms can no longer take the strain of magic coursing through them, and those who are the most ancient and venerated grow hotter, and hotter, and eventually explode into ash.

THE DARKNESS

Hunger: Hunger itself.

Prime power: Darkness.

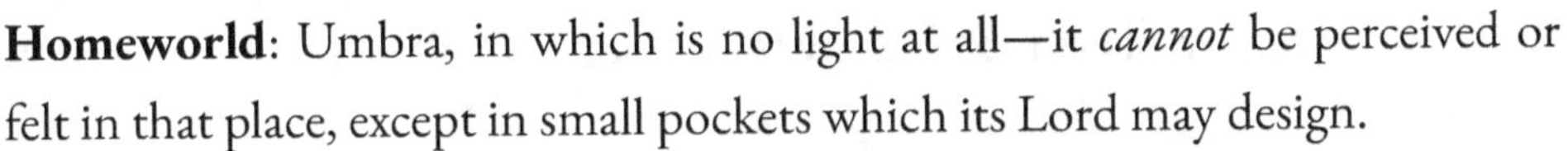

Homeworld: Umbra, in which is no light at all—it *cannot* be perceived or felt in that place, except in small pockets which its Lord may design.

Those who are of the Darkness *hunger.* Most eat; some collect. There are those who can and do devour anything, including plague, radiation, and the dead. The Fey, in particular, are much prized, their magic unique for whatever the Throne and Scepter do to it before sending it back out.

Toward the end of their natural lifespan, their own forms can no longer satisfy their aching, empty need. Those who are the most ancient and venerated grow more shadowed, less substantial, and eventually fade like mist in morning sun..

THE GUARDIANS

Hunger: Protection.

Prime power: Resistance.

World: Officially, none.

Guardians are driven to protect. This need can attach itself to anything; there are sphinxes still guarding tombs deep underground, where they will remain until they die.

Something terrible happened in the First War, and those Guardians who remain are uniformly mad. Most still function amoing the Peoples, but rumors say the most powerful are locked away for the safety of all.

The Guardians are wildly varied in terms of natural lifespan. Some fairies live months; dragsons can live for centuries. The Saqalu, who inspired the four-winged symbol of the People of the Guardians, did not age.

However, no one lives forever; the Saqalu are gone, now called the Hashritu, the Broken, and are lost to all but memory.

THE FEY

Hunger: Curiosity.

Prime power: Creation.

World: The Silver Dawning, divided between the Seelie Scepter and Unseelie Throne.

The Fey, flighty and mercurial, often discover and build only to abandon. They are in part driven by an unnatural need to reclaim the magic stolen from them; all their power, from birth, is channeled until the Throne and Scepter, there to be distributed and wielded as needed to keep their People alive. Mostly, though, the Fey are driven by curiosity. *Can I make it work?* is eye-rollingly funny as a trope.

Alone among the Seven Peoples, the Fey must seek magic outside of themselves, or starve; it is a skill learned to weave it from others, from emotion or intimacy, from applause or anguish. Toward the end of their natural lifespan, they lose the ability to process these stolen strands of power. Their bodies grow cool, and still; they become smooth, pale stone, without blemish, and without life. When Fey reach the natural end of their lives, they leave behind them soulless statues of themselves, echoes of the beauty they once held.

THE DREAM

Hunger: Dreams.

Prime power: The influence and digestion of the unconscious mind.

World: The Plane of Dreams, guarded by ambulant trees, home to complete silence.

The Dream are rarely seen. They withrew from the horrors of the First War, and now dwell between realms, living in the walls that divide wake and sleep. Some taste nightmares and build them to madness; some share sweetness and encourage hope.

Their lifespans are unknown. The end of their natural existence is unknown. Inheritors of uneasy flesh, they have lost the ability to manifest sharply in our world for more than moments of time, and it remains unclear if they can ever rejoin those who truly live.

THE KIN

Hunger: Varied.

Prime power: Varied.

World: All worlds, but primarily the human Earth.

The majority of Kin appear human, and are the source of all tales of humans who wield such power. They aren't one thing or another, neither fish nor flesh nor good red herring, but the legacy of many Peoples, who nevertheless rarely recognize Kin as their own. Due to unpredictable genetics, Kin powers vary wildly.

The Kin were once trafficked. They themselves could be used to increase the numbers of an identifiable People progeny, and so Kin were taken, used, and discardded—until nine brave families stepped forward to claim the Kin's place upon the Great Wheel. Lin, Blackwood, Lester, Sims, Doe, Yang, Bard, Roth, and Williams: may their names never be forgotten! Those who had no home now do, a People and a power and presence to be respected.

THE EVER-DYING

Hunger: Discovery.

Prime power: None.

World: Earth.

From the viewpoint of the magical among the Mythos, humans are dying from the moment they're born. They are horrifyingly short-lived. Anything can kill them; worse tet, they have no magic, and can neither wield nor perceive its use.

They can, however, reproduce at a rate rarely seen outside of rabbits.

Notte, Naktam who chose the Peoples, the Lord of the Night Whispers, regards the Ever-Dying as precious, for only they can become his children. His intervention and protection enabled their growth, and ensured their place on the Wheel even though they have no magic.

THE LOST

Hunger: Unknown.

Prime power: Terrible.

World: Unknown.

"Lost" is a misnomer. Tthe Scepter and the Fey saw that many did not fit into the sillos of the Seven Peoples of the Earth, and so tried to claim them. After all, their magic could continue to power the Silver Dawning.

This turned out to be a bad idea. Some beings could be claimed, yes, and their magic stolen, but the rest...

Gods. Demons. Psychopomps. Those things which eschew names and descriptions as worthless and ill-fitted. Many live outside of reality in the Void; too, are those who are not native to Earth, even as it was before it shattered. Of these, less said is better said. They are frightening, for none know what drives them.

AMONG THE MYTHOS, WHO ARE YOU?

No one is defined by their People, any more than an ethnicity or culture determines who a person is, but it does influence environment and options. Understanding this ancient rubric is the first step into this world, and explains why these beings always introduce themselves thus: **Among the Mythos, I am [People,] called [name.] Who are you?**

LEXICON

IN WHICH IS LISTED NAMES AND TERMS

CHARACTERS

Bran: Prince of the People of the Darkness. Of the Shadow's Breath, he is powerful and beautiful—though for *some* reason, he prefers appearing in his human guise instead of as his enormous, seven-foot-tall, horned, brick-red self.

Jonathan Sumeragi: Jonathan is a Night-Child and an impossibility. He is a seer, which means magic, which means he was Kin and not human—and Kin *cannot* be come vampires. At least, normally, they can't. He's the third Kin in all of history to be successfully *made*, and no one understands why it worked. He expresses his future-sight Still through his paintings. Recovering from a life time of abuse at Ravena's hand, he denies his abilities and downplays his skill, but it should be noted that he has *never been wrong*.

Elijah: Elijah Tuttle exists in an uneasy place: the creation of a Night-Child from an *actual* child is utterly forbidden, but here he is. He lived in London as a contemporary of Charles Dickens, and had enough (just) to eat, a couple sets of clothes, and one very strange skill: he could seemingly hear dead people speaking to him through his mother's harp. Ravena is always trying to recreate her accidental masterpiece of Jonathan, so she took a risk and turned him. However, Kin cannot be made into Night-Children, and it turned out the harp was magic, not the boy. He was turned successfully, but only after he'd been *made* did Ravena realize what had happened. He's a clever, bitter little boy, trapped forever in a young body.

Liza: Elizabeth Oshun Thomas is a Night-Child. She was 28 years old when she was made, born and raised in east London. She's tall, black, and striking. Liza is fairly new vampire, and a remarkable communicator, which has caught the attention of Ravena. She's technically five generations down the line from Notte, and her maker is Arabelle.

Mer'Qel: A warrior who single-handedly united the clans of warring mer-people in the Pacific. She owns a unique collar that allows her to change her shape, and a luminescent white fur wrap that allows her to breathe air without weakening.

Notte: Naktam; Night-King; Nox Aeterna; He Who Walks Unhindered; King of Blood; the Blood King; Lord of the Night Whispers; Notte the Unending; the Mortal's Doom; and of course, just *Night*. He's one of the oldest living beings among the Mythos. The father of all vampires (or Night-Children, as they're called), he's a mystery; no one knows where the heck he came from. From all appearances, he cannot be killed—even in those times when when he wanted to die. Although Night-Children are transformed humans, they do not fall into the category of Kin, but thanks to their hunger, are of The Darkness.

Salome: A Night-Child with an unusual skill for dancing. Notte chose her, though he did not personally make her. She was born in 1900, was made into a Night-Child at the age of 22, and still maintains her flapper style just because she loves it. She's a little otherwordly; her hobby is actually designing custom scents for perfumes and other uses, and she's very, very good at it.

Ravena: A Night-Child, and Notte's oldest surviving offspring. She's immensely powerful, and through conflict, love, and loss, has been granted the right to run her Night-Child family completely outside of Notte's rules. The tension between the two defies description, leading to absurd and often cruel choices aimed in Notte's direction.

Seishirou: A Samurai once, deeply devoted to his feudal lord. Caught up in war before the Edo period, Seishirou protected his lord until the very end, and almost died for it. Ravena, who'd been haunting the island of Japan for a while, found his loyalty fascinating and his honor laughable, and decided to make him her own personal assassin.

Terrance: One of Notte's "first-born," which is to say a vampire Notte himself turned. Terrance is Irish, born sometime in the 1300s. His skill, anger, and cleverness sealed his fate in more than one way: Terrance was sentenced to death by beheading, but the night before his execution, Notte came to his cell and made him an offer. Terrance took it: he became one of the Night-Children , accepting Notte's authority in exchange for preserving his life. Terrance loves Notte fiercely, and possibly loves nothing and no one else. He's Notte's *knife*, the assigned assassin of the Night-Children, and the only one sanctioned to take life regularly.

TERMS

Kobold: Kobolds are tiny, fairly weak creatures, with magic usually best used in domestic tasks. They are the Lost, unclaimed, but nobody much minds. If they're paid well, they're happy to watch any home and cook any food. Betraying them, however, leads to years of curses and spoiled milk and moldy bread.

Gargoyles: Beings seemingly made of stone, of the Lost. They are born from mountains where much blood was spilled, and their own blood is gray. They are not, generally, intelligent, but are capable of following orders.

Night-Child: The source of all "vampire" rumors, Night-Children are an ancient and frightening breed, and very difficult to kill. They must be made from humans; with only a few exceptions, any magic in the blood prevents transformation. Once they are *made*, transformed into something far different from human, several key details remain: one, no matter ethnic heritage, all of them have the same green eyes, which have a tendency to glow. Two, they all carry a hunger they call the Beast—a mad bloodlust, which, if ignored, drives the Night-Child insane. They must drink human blood, though it does not need to be to the death. Three, they all inherit an ability they call *going to dust*. It's called "dust" because that's what it looks like—dust motes swirling in sunlight. It isn't dust, however. It's impossible to retain, control, or stop; it can pass through any solid surface, and travel at unbelievable speeds. No one fully understands how this works. Notte controls his family strictly. Ravena, not so much, though even they may not cross certain lines.

Want more? There is a full wiki on <u>https://ruthannereid.com/</u>. Enjoy!

NO ONE WRITES ALONE

This book wouldn't have been possible without Miko, Celine, and Bennett. They're the best cheerleaders I could ever imagine, and their feedback is and has been critical to the development of my world.

Ilana Waters is an unexpected joy, helping me relish the "vampire family drama" facet of this tale.

J.M. Frey is my writing sister, and someday, we are going to do that hug and it will be *awesome*.

Cameron kept me going more times than he knows. His little tweets and mentions have pulled me out of numerous funks.

My husband is my inspiration, my encouragement, and my best friend, and just typing about him makes me smile. We'll find that special place someday, my love. I know it in my gut.

ABOUT THE AUTHOR

A bestselling author, Ruthanne Reid has led panels on world-building, taught courses on plot and character development, and been the keynote speaker for the Write Practice Retreat. Author of nine books and dozens of short stories, she makes daily videos to help other creatives get unblocked and into a healthy habit of creation.

Ruthanne has lived in her head since childhood, when she used up her mom's red typewriter ribbon writing a story about a pony princess and a genocidal snake-kingdom. When she isn't reading, writing, or reading about writing, Ruthanne enjoys old cartoons with her husband and cats, and dreams of living on an island far, far away.

Find her on: https://youtube.com/ruthannereid | https://patreon.com/ruthannereid/ | https://ruthannereid.com/

www.ingramcontent.com/pod-product-compliance
Lightning Source LLC
Chambersburg PA
CBHW072119150726
47999CB00005B/2032